The Snow WMBLE

For Annabel Bryce
K.R.

For Tilly
N.P.

Bloomsbury Publishing, London, New Delhi, New York and Sydney

First published by Bloomsbury Publishing Plc in October 2012
50 Bedford Square, London, WC1B 3DP

First published in Great Britain in 1975 by Ernest Benn Ltd

The Snow Womble text copyright © Elisabeth Beresford 1975
The Snow Womble revised text copyright © Elisabeth Beresford, Kate Robertson
and Marcus Robertson 2012
Illustrations copyright © Nick Price 2012

The moral rights of the authors and illustrator have been asserted

A CIP catalogue record for this book is available from the British Library

ISBN 978 1 4088 3424 4

1 3 5 7 9 10 8 6 4 2

Printed in Italy by Lego S.p.A., Vicenza

www.bloomsbury.com
www.thewomblesbooks.com

The Snow WOMBLE

Elisabeth Beresford

Illustrated by Nick Price

BLOOMSBURY

LONDON   NEW DELHI   NEW YORK   SYDNEY

It had been snowing all night on Wimbledon Common. When the Wombles came out of their burrow to start tidying up, everything looked quite different. The Wombles just stopped and stared.

'Doesn't the common look clean?' said Bungo. 'And isn't the snow white!'

'It looks just like ice cream,' said Orinoco,
who was very greedy. 'I wonder if it tastes as nice?'
And he ate some. It tasted so cold it made his fur stand
up on end and his teeth chatter.

'What you need to do, Orinoco, is to run about,' said Tomsk.
'That will soon warm you up. Come for a slide on this old tin tray.
It will be fun!'

But Orinoco thought the soft snow was much better for sleeping on than sliding. He began to make a snow bed with his paws.

'I've just had a better idea,' said Bungo. 'Let's make a Snow Womble! Let's make it look like Great Uncle Bulgaria. Come and help me, Orinoco!'

But Orinoco wasn't listening.
He was curled up fast asleep.
So Bungo started to make
the Snow Womble on his own.

He made the body and
then the head. He put on a
shawl and then a hat.

Soon the Snow Womble began to look
very, very, **very** like Great Uncle Bulgaria.
'I just need some spectacles,' said Bungo.
He was very pleased with his work.

Meanwhile, Tomsk was having
a lovely time sliding down
all the snowy slopes.

'Ooh,' said Tomsk, as he made himself go in a wiggly line instead of a straight one. 'This is exciting!'

Bungo finished making the Great Uncle Bulgaria Snow Womble. He was so proud of it, he wanted to find another Womble to come and look at it. So off he went.

It was no good asking Orinoco because he was still fast asleep. Orinoco was dreaming about ice cream: lots and lots of it, with cherries and strawberries and swirls of cream on top.

'Mmm,' he sighed happily, and he settled himself even more comfortably in the snow.

Just then, Tomsk decided it would be more fun if Bungo came sliding with him. *I'll slide down here,* he thought, *and give him a surprise!*

Faster and faster he went.

Suddenly he saw Great Uncle Bulgaria standing at the bottom of the slope.

'Get out of the way, please get out of the way!'
shouted Tomsk, waving his arms.

But Great Uncle Bulgaria
didn't move at all.
  'Oh dear. Oh help, someone, please!
This tray hasn't got any brakes!'
shouted Tomsk again.

He tried to stop but it was no good. He kept going faster and **faster** and **faster** and Great Uncle Bulgaria *still* didn't move.

Tomsk shut his eyes.

And the next minute . . .

Tomsk went flying into the air and landed upside-down in the snow. *Oof!*

Tomsk slowly opened his eyes.

What had happened to Great Uncle Bulgaria? All he could see was a shawl and a hat.

Tomsk gulped.

And then he heard a gruff voice say, 'What are you doing lying there with your mouth open, you silly young Womble?'

Tomsk turned round and there was Great Uncle Bulgaria standing in the doorway of the burrow.

Tomsk stared and stared and *stared*. He could hardly believe his eyes! But it was very nice to see that he had not hurt Great Uncle Bulgaria after all.

'What has been going on?' asked Great Uncle Bulgaria sternly.

Tomsk tried to explain but he kept getting more and more muddled. 'I thought it was you . . . I mean, I thought you were . . . oh dear,' said Tomsk.

But Great Uncle Bulgaria was a very clever old Womble and he soon realised what had happened.

'So some young Womble made a Snow Womble that looked like me!' he said with a twinkle in his eye. 'That gives me an idea. Off you go to the burrow, Tomsk. It's nearly time for tea.'

As soon as Tomsk had gone, Great Uncle Bulgaria went and stood exactly where the Snow Womble had been. He stood very still indeed.
Soon Bungo came running up.

Bungo hadn't found any other Wombles to admire his Snow Womble so he went over to Orinoco, who was *still* fast asleep.

'Wake up, Orinoco, you lazy Womble,' said Bungo. 'Come and look at the lovely Snow Womble I've made. It's the best Snow Womble in the whole world. Oh do wake up.'

And he took hold of both his friend's paws and tugged hard.

Slowly Orinoco opened his eyes, and blinked and yawned and stretched.

Then he got up and went to look at the Snow Womble. It really was very, **very**, **very** like Great Uncle Bulgaria.

'It *is* a good Snow Womble,' said Orinoco. 'It looks just as cross as Great Uncle Bulgaria does sometimes.'

And he started to laugh.

'And just as strict as Great Uncle Bulgaria is sometimes,' said Bungo.

And he started to laugh too.

The two Wombles laughed and laughed and **laughed**.
They laughed so much they didn't see that Great Uncle Bulgaria was shaking as he tried not to laugh too.

Just you wait, young Wombles, he thought.

'Of course I look cross *sometimes*. And of course I am strict *sometimes*, when I have to deal with silly young Wombles like you!' said Great Uncle Bulgaria very loudly.

Bungo and Orinoco were so surprised at hearing the Snow Womble speak, they both sat down *plop* in the snow.

'Now then, young Wombles,' said Great Uncle Bulgaria. 'Get back on your paws and pick up all this rubbish. You had better hurry or you'll be late for tea.'

Bungo and Orinoco were very shocked that the Snow Womble had turned into the real Great Uncle Bulgaria. They were even more shocked at the thought of missing their tea.

Without another word, Bungo and Orinoco picked up the Snow Womble's shawl and his spectacles and his hat. Just as they had finished tidying up, Tomsk came out of the burrow.

'Hurry up!' he said. 'It's tea time and we are going to have iced cakes and real ice cream.'

And Orinoco and Bungo hurried into
the burrow as fast as they could.

It started to snow again and the flakes
began to settle on Great Uncle Bulgaria's fur.
*I really shall turn into a Snow Womble
if I stand out here any longer,* he thought.
He gently shook the snow off and
walked back to the burrow.

Inside the burrow, all the Wombles were enjoying a delicious tea.

'If only you could have seen your faces, young Wombles,' said Great Uncle Bulgaria, as Bungo and Orinoco tucked into huge slices of iced nettle-cake. 'Ha, ha! I haven't had so much fun in the snow since I was a young Womble!'

CAIRNGORM
MACWOMBLE THE TERRIBLE

But that's another story . . .

Goodbye! See you soon!

Bungo

Tomsk

Great Uncle Bulgar